SUPER SPECS

by Laura Driscoll
Illustrated by Barry Gott

Kane Press, Inc.
New York

Book Design/Art Direction: Roberta Pressel

Library of Congress Cataloging-in-Publication Data

Gott Barry.
    Super specs / by Laura Driscoll; illustrated by Barry Gott.
      p. cm. — (Math matters.)
    "Number patterns—grades: K-2."
    Summary: On a family car trip, Molly uses mathematics to convince her younger brother
that she has x-ray vision.
    ISBN 1-57565-145-9 (pbk. : alk. paper)
    [1. Eyeglasses—Fiction. 2. Brothers and sisters—Fiction. 3. Mathematics—Fiction.
4. Automobile travel—Fiction.]
    I. Gott, Barry, ill. II. Title. III. Series.
    PZ7.D79Su 2005
    [E]—dc22
                        2004016959

10 9 8 7 6 5 4 3 2 1

First published in the United States of America in 2005 by Kane Press, Inc.
Printed in Hong Kong.

MATH MATTERS is a registered trademark of Kane Press, Inc.

www.kanepress.com

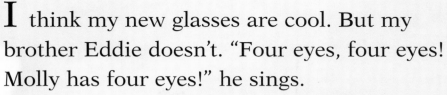

I think my new glasses are cool. But my brother Eddie doesn't. "Four eyes, four eyes! Molly has four eyes!" he sings.

We're on our way to Super Funland. I said we should leave Eddie home, but my parents wouldn't do it.

"Eddie!" Dad says. "Don't call Molly names."

"It's okay, Dad," I tell him. "Eddie's not bothering me."

But Eddie *is* bugging me. I just don't want him to know it.

So I pretend not to see him make googly-glasses faces.

I stare out the window, even though there's nothing to look at but trees and the sign for Exit 5.

Eddie draws a silly cartoon of me on his sketch pad. I just keep pretending not to notice. We pass Exit 6.

"Dad," I ask, "what's the Super Funland exit?"

"Exit 10," he replies.

Yikes! Four more exits to go—lots of time for Eddie to torture me.

"Hey!" Eddie yells. "You look like Solar Man with your new glasses." He points to his Solar Man comic book and gives me a wise-guy grin. "Too bad *yours* don't have x-ray vision!"

I grit my teeth. "There's Exit 7," I say to myself.

Eddie sticks his comic book right in my face. I don't say anything. I just look for Exit 8.

How far is it between exits, anyway? It feels like forever.

At last I see the sign.

What is the next number in this pattern?
5, 6, 7, 8, ?

Hurry up, Exit 9!

If I don't get away from smart-mouth Eddie soon, I'm going to explode.

I let out a big sigh.

I've got to make him quit all his annoying talk about glasses—and x-ray vision.

Then I get an idea.

I'll make Eddie think that my glasses *do* give me x-ray vision. *That* will change his tune.

I work out a plan. It won't be easy.

But I think I can pull it off.

We stop at a gas station. Mom takes Eddie and me to get snacks while Dad fills up the car.

"Hey, Eddie," I say, "want to play I Spy?" Eddie likes car games even more than teasing me.

"Great!" he says.

We drive off. I squint and look out the window.
"I spy something green with the number 9 on it,"
I say.

I'm just pretending. All the exit signs are
green—and I know Exit 9 is coming up. But
Eddie doesn't. The sign is still a few miles down
the road.

"There's a 9!"
Eddie yells. He's
pointing at a car's
license plate.

"That's not green,"
I tell him. "Keep
looking!"

I try not to laugh.

We drive over a hill, around a bend, and
past a cornfield. Finally Eddie sees the sign
for Exit 9.

"There it is!" he exclaims.

"Yep," I say. "That's it."

Eddie does a little dance in his seat.
Then he looks at me. "How could you see
that sign from all the way back at the gas
station?"

I shrug. "X-ray vision."

Eddie snorts. "Yeah, right," he says.

A few minutes later we get to Exit 10 and pull off the highway. We're at Super Funland!

"It's so crowded," Mom complains.

Mom's right. The parking lot is almost
full. We drive around and around, looking
for a space.

At last we find one—far away from the
park entrance.

"Remember—we're parked in Section 5," Dad says. He points to a tall sign near our spot.
"Let's go!" says Eddie.

We walk past the signs for Section 4, then 3, then 2. We're almost at the entrance!

Out of the corner of my eye, I see Eddie frowning. "You don't have x-ray vision," he says. "It's impossible."

But he doesn't sound so sure.

"Impossible?" I say, and smile.

I've got another trick up my sleeve. This one is sure to freak Eddie out.

"See that?" I point to the sign up ahead. "What does it say?"

Eddie squints. "I can't read it from here."

What is the next number in this pattern?
5, 4, 3, 2, ?

I push my glasses up on my nose.

"There's a big number 1 on the other side of that sign."

"You're just guessing," Eddie grumbles.

"I guess we'll see," I tell him.

We walk by the sign. Eddie sees I'm right. He's so amazed, he stops in his tracks. Then he runs up to Mom and Dad.

"Can I get glasses like Molly's?" he begs. "Please?"

I can't help giggling. Eddie fell for my trick, all right. But it's time to let him in on the joke.

I wait until we get to Candy Village. "These aren't really x-ray glasses, Eddie," I say. "There's a *pattern* to the exit numbers on the highway. Same goes for the parking-lot signs."

"A pattern?" asks Eddie. "What does *that* mean?"

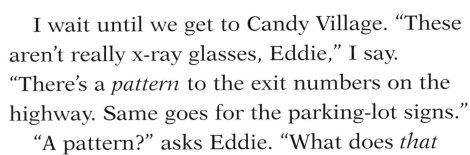

"Check out the houses on this side of the street," I tell him. "See how each one has a number? That first house is number 2. The next is 4. Then 6. Then 8. So what will the next one be?"

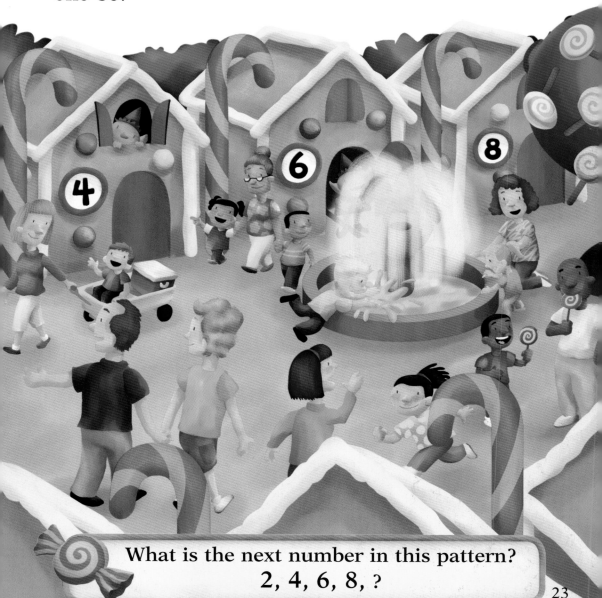

What is the next number in this pattern?
2, 4, 6, 8, ?

"Number 10?" says Eddie.

Right after we pass the lollipop tree, Eddie spots number 10 Sweet Tooth Lane.

"Wow!" he shouts. "I have x-ray vision, too!"

Eddie looks for number patterns all day.
He finds them on the Ferris wheel.

What is the next number in this pattern?
10, 8, 6, 4, ?

He spots them at the boat ride.

What is the next number in this pattern?
1, 3, 5, 7, ?

And he shows off again at the game arcade.

One prize doesn't have a number. But when
Eddie wins, he calls out, "Seven, please!"

Eddie knows what the prize number is, even
though he can't see it.

Eddie doesn't tease me on the ride home. He's too busy calling out exit numbers. "Exit 5, coming up!" he says.

We've already passed Exits 8, 7, and 6. Yep. Eddie really has the hang of number patterns.

But I have one last trick.

"Mom," I say. "Can we stop at the Ice Cream Depot up ahead?"

"Where?" asks Mom. "All I see is highway."

"Just wait," I tell her.

"There it is!" Eddie yells.

We can all see the giant cone.

"Next stop, Ice Cream Depot!" Dad announces.

Eddie follows me out of the car. "That was no number trick!" he blurts out. "How did you know the Depot would be here?"

I push my super specs up on my nose and shrug.

"Easy," I say. "There's been one at every exit!"

ᴺᵁᴹᴮᴱᴿ PATTERNS CHART

You can be a number pattern expert!

Every number pattern has a rule. The numbers in a pattern are in a special order.

The **RULE** tells you about the pattern.

RULE: Count forward 2.

2, 4, 6, 8

Think:
2, 3, 4, 5,
6, 7, 8

Think:
9, 8, 7, 6,
5, 4, 3

RULE: Count backward 2.

9, 7, 5, 3

Look at the number pattern.

Name the **RULE**.

What's the next number in the pattern?

1. 9, 8, 7, 6, ?   **2.** 1, 3, 5, 7, ?

3. 2, 3, 4, 5, ?   **4.** 10, 8, 6, 4, ?

[Answers: 1. RULE: Count backward 1; 5; 2. RULE: Count forward 2; 9; 3. RULE: Count forward 1; 6; 4. RULE: Count backward 2; 2]